For my perfect pineapple, Jessie –
love Mum
V.F.
For my son, Joel
with all my love
A.B.

Oliver's Fruit Salad
by Vivian French and Alison Bartlett
British Library Cataloguing in Publication Data
A catalogue record of this book is available from the British Library

ISBN 0 340 704527 (HB)
ISBN 0 340 704535 (PB)

First edition published 1998
10 9 8 7 6 5 4

Published by Hodder Children's Books,
a division of Hodder Headline plc,
338 Euston Road, London NW1 3BH

Printed in Belgium

Oliver's Fruit Salad

Vivian French

Illustrated by
Alison Bartlett

Hodder
Children's
Books

A division of Hodder Headline plc

Oliver was eating his breakfast. He looked at his cereal and put down his spoon.
"When I was staying with Grandpa," he said, "I helped him pick scrunchy red apples every morning."
"How lovely," said Mum.

When Mum made herself a cup of coffee Oliver shook his head
at his drink of blackcurrant juice.
"At Grandpa's house I saw REAL blackcurrants. Gran let me
top and tail them. She put them in a pie."
"Goodness me," said Mum.

At lunch time Oliver's Mum looked in the cupboard.
"Shall we have tinned pears?" she asked.
Oliver sniffed.
"Grandpa GROWS pears," he said. "He doesn't eat pears out of tins.
He grows pears on trees."
"Lucky Grandpa," said Mum.

After lunch Mum got their coats.
"Let's go shopping," she said.
"Grandpa doesn't go shopping," said Oliver. "He grows
EVERYTHING in his garden."
"Hurry up," said Mum. "Put your coat on."
"All right," sighed Oliver.

In the supermarket Mum went to look at the jams.
Oliver told her about Grandpa's WONDERFUL cherries
and strawberries and plums.
"Oliver," said Mum, "look over there."
"Why?" asked Oliver.

"Look!" said Mum.

Oliver looked. He saw apples and blackcurrants and pears.

He saw cherries and strawberries and plums.

"H'm," said Oliver. "I still think Grandpa's fruit is better."

"What about bananas and grapes?" said Mum.

"Grandpa could grow them if he wanted to," Oliver said firmly.

Mum pulled up a shopping trolley and filled it with fruit.
"I've never seen one of those in Grandpa's garden," Oliver said,
pointing at a pineapple.
"We'll buy one then," Mum said, and she did.

Oliver helped Mum carry all the bags home.
They piled up the fruit on the kitchen table.
"Now," said Mum. "You can eat an apple. Or a pear.
Or a plum. It's not in a jar or a tin. It's all fresh,
so help yourself."

Oliver shook his head.
"No, thank you," he said. "I just HELPED Grandpa.
I didn't EAT any of the fruit. I don't LIKE fruit."
Mum stared. "Oh, OLIVER!"

The door bell rang. Oliver rushed to open the door.
It was Gran and Grandpa.
"Hullo!" said Oliver. "Come and see what we've got!"

Gran and Grandpa looked at all the fruit.
"FRUIT SALAD!" said Grandpa.
"What's that?" asked Oliver.
"Something very special," said Gran.
"We'll make it together."

Gran, Oliver, Mum and Grandpa chopped up the fruit.
When it was all in a big blue bowl, Oliver smiled.
"It looks very pretty," he said.

Mum put out three bowls.
"Where's mine?" asked Oliver.
"You don't like fruit," said Mum.

"I like fruit salad," said Oliver, and he had three helpings.
"SCRUMMY!" he said. He licked his spoon thoughtfully.
"But I bet if it was all out of Grandpa's garden it would be even
SCRUMMIER!"

And even Mum laughed.